WALT DISNEY'S
NOAH'S ARK

STORY ADAPTED BY
MONIQUE PETERSON

PICTURES BY
THE WALT DISNEY STUDIOS
ADAPTED BY
CAMPBELL GRANT

A WELCOME BOOK

DISNEY
EDITIONS

New York

Father Noah had no time to waste. A flood was coming!
God told him to make haste and gather wood, then measure it,
cut it, and bind it with pitch.

Birds squawked with excitement and flew through the skies.
"Ark! Ark! Noah's building an ark!" shrieked the magpie.

The birds spread the news to their friends on the African plains. "I've never seen enough rain for a flood," said the rhinoceros with a grunt.

"Listen!" cried the blue jay throughout the Asian highlands.
"Noah is building an ark to save us from a great flood!"
"Impossible!" snarled the tiger.

"God told Noah the rain will fall for forty days and forty nights," chirped the warbler.

"That's all right." The gorilla smiled. "A little rain won't bother me at all."

"Two by two by two," the parrot proclaimed to the hippopotamus. "Noah wants pairs of every animal to enter the ark two by two."

The possums hanging in the treetops had nothing to say but "Zzzz-Zzzz-Zzzz."

"We need our banana trees," said the swinging monkeys in the rain forest. "In forty days we'll surely starve!"

"Don't worry," twittered the sparrows. "We'll have plenty to eat. Noah has promised us berries and nuts and fruits and grains. There will be honey and nectar, too."

And the birds spread the word across the lands both near and far, from the highest mountains to the Arctic shores.

"Food!" squawked the seagull. "The ark is filled with food enough for all!"

"Mmm!" roared the great white polar bears. "Let's hurry off this iceberg and go straight there!"

"Food!" rattled the kingfisher near the northern woodland caves.

"Great!" growled the grizzly bears. "Combs of wild honey are too good to resist."

The wild mustangs galloped across the desert plains.
They heard the news, too.

"Wild oats!" whinnied the mare. They ran to join
the others.

When the news spread to the marshlands, the elephants tossed their trunks high and trumpeted, "Hurrah!" And with their big strong legs they stomp-stomp-stomped all the way to the ark.

The ground thundered with the pounding feet of wild beasts. The field mice heard it and scurried to meet the others. "Please leave some seeds and grains for us!" they yipped.

"Berries and worms, too!" chirruped the robin redbreasts.
High up in the treetops the squirrels chattered and barked.
"Noah said we can feast on acorns while we travel on the ark!"
In the briar patches down below, the jackrabbits and hares
heard the good news. "Sweet carrots and lettuce!" they
twittered, and hopped happily on their way.

The growing parade trotted and trampled and flew their way toward the ark.

The tabby cats crouched in the fields and perked their ears with delight. "Delicious milk and cream!" they purred.

But the possums dozed dreamily on . . . "Zzzz-Zzzz-Zzzz."

Two by two they came, from the littlest of bugs to the biggest of bears, just as Noah had declared. Aardvarks, badgers, and Mongolian yaks; ermines and jaguars with spots on their backs; foxes, chipmunks, and kangaroos, too; ladybugs and butterflies bluer than blue; monkeys, moose, and raccoons

with striped tails; lions, llamas, peacocks, and quails; turkeys,
turtles, and animals with horns, like rhinos, cows, and unicorns;
dingoes, newts, spiders, and snails; great apes, and rabbits with
big fluffy tails; waddling penguins, wriggly worms . . . they
entered the ark in one massive swarm!

"Hurry!" urged Noah, for the skies were growing black. And the last of the herd—from warthogs to zebras—ran up the plank through the doors of the ark.

Father Noah checked his list and marked off each pair
as the first crack of thunder drummed through the skies.
"Oh, no!" he cried. "The possums are missing!" So the
sharp-eyed eagles flew with great speed, and brought
back the possums, who still were asleep. Then, as soon
as Noah bolted the big door shut, the whole sky opened
up . . . and it POURED, POURED, POURED!

The rains came down, down, down, and the waters rose up, up, up, until soon the ark floated higher than the tallest treetop. And down below, where birds once flew, swam schools of fish and a big shark, too!

The storm outside whipped the ark to and fro with the waves. Each rise and dip of the seesawing ark twisted and tangled the giraffes' necks in knots. The tigers felt seasick and moaned in despair.

The nighttime was the hardest for the chickens, chickadees, and hares. The mountain lions and foxes chased them. And the owls and the ospreys swooped low over their heads, keeping them awake the whole night.

But then in the morning when the predators tried to snooze, the rooster woke them with a "Cock-a-doodle-doo!"

The days were miserable for most everyone on board. The camels missed the feeling of the sand between their toes, and the flamingos had no water in which to wade. The antelope missed loping and the beavers missed gnawing on wood. But the possums didn't miss a thing . . . they just snoozed and snoozed and snoozed.

On the fortieth night after the fortieth day, the heavens cleared and at last the rain stopped. But the waters still covered the earth as far as the eye could see. So God sent the winds to clear the waters away. They drifted for days until . . . BUMP! The ark landed on the tip of Mount Ararat.

When the winds stopped blowing and the ark stopped rocking, Noah opened the windows and looked all about. But all he saw was water, so he sent out a dove to scout for land. She flew far and wide and returned only to coo, "I'm tired, and must rest. I could find no place to perch my feet or build myself a nest."

Seven days passed, and the animals grew restless and weary. So Noah sent out the dove again and prayed that she'd return in a hurry. The dove flew off, and to everyone's relief, she returned with the gift of an olive branch in her beak. "Land!" Noah shouted. "Praise be to God! Let's disembark and let the animals run wild!"

Noah, his wife, and their sons, Shem, Ham, and Japheth, climbed down from the mountain and stepped foot on dry earth. The geese circled high, honking, "Home! Home! Home!" And the animals roamed to the far corners of the land to start up new families in forest, fields, snow, and sand.

God blessed Noah and his children and said, "Have many children, so that your descendants will live all over the earth. I promise you—and all living things—all birds and all animals that came out of the ark with you, that a great flood will never come again."